LOVELY, LOVELY PIRATE GOLD

First published 2007
Evans Brothers Limited
2A Portman Mansions
Chiltern St
London W1U 6NR

British Library Cataloguing in Publication Data

Anderson, Scoular
        Lovely lovely pirate gold. - (Zig zag)
        1. Pirates - Juvenile fiction 2. Treasure troves - Juvenile
        fiction 3. Maps - Juvenile fiction 4. Children's stories
        I. Title
        823.9'14[J]

ISBN-10: 0 237 53166 6 (hb)
13 digit ISBN: 978 0237 53166 9
ISBN-10: 0 237 53170 4 (pb)
13 digit ISBN: 978 0237 53170 6

Printed in China

Series Editor: Nick Turpin
Design: Robert Walster
Production: Jenny Mulvanny

LOVELY, LOVELY PIRATE GOLD

by Scoular Anderson

Evans

When the pirate captain
opened his chest...

...looking for socks and
an itchy vest...

...he found – a map!

He ran to his crew…

"You know what to do
with this wonderful clue –
it's time to hunt for treasure."

So they sailed away…

14

...to a wide, sandy bay...

13

...where they all
lent a hand...

14

...to dig in the sand.

The sand piled up as they dug for loot…

16

...but they found no treasure,
just a smelly old boot!

19

The captain cried, "It's just
not fair!"
Then stamped his foot and
pulled his hair.

The cabin boy looked at
the map…

22

...first like this, then like that.

23

At last he told them with
a frown,
"The treasure map was
upside down!"

24

They raced away to
dig again.

This time the captain did not complain!

29

Then each pirate wore a smile,
when each pirate had a pile
of lovely, lovely pirate gold.